Newton, Nell, and Barney.

Someday
I Want
to Be ...

This book is dedicated
to all children and
with much love
to Henry

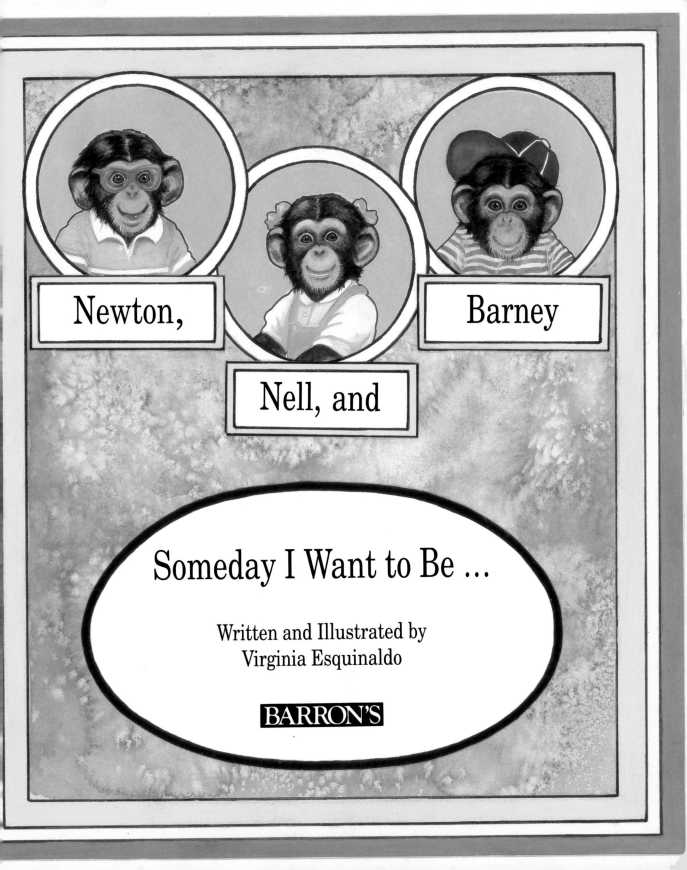

One afternoon, Newton, Nell, and Barney were outside playing. "Did you ever wonder what you would like to be someday?" asked Newton.

"Yes," said Barney. "It's fun pretending to be a grown-up!"

"Let's play a game called SOMEDAY!" Nell exclaimed. "We'll take turns telling each other what we want to be someday!"

Barney remembered helping Mama bake a cake. It was messy, but fun! And the cake tasted so good!
..."That's what I could be!" thought Barney.

Someday I could become a...

BAKER!"

Nell was swinging in the backyard.
She stopped to take a deep breath.
The roses smelled wonderful!

"A garden is a terrific place to be," she thought. "When I grow up, I'll plant lots of flowers. Someday I want to be a...

GARDENER!"

Newton was very curious. He spent hours outdoors looking under rocks or digging in the dirt. Whenever he found an interesting plant or animal, he took its picture.

"Someday, when I grow up," Newton thought, "I could take my camera all around the world and take pictures of my discoveries! I could become a...

PHOTOGRAPHER."

Mama gave Newton, Nell, and Barney some old boxes.
With crayons and scissors they changed the boxes
into different things.

Newton drew many little
windows on the boxes.
Then, he placed one on
top of the other. "Look
and see my skyscraper!"
he said. "Someday
I want to be a…
BUILDER!"

Nell colored a big box white and cut out a door and windows. Then she taped a small flag over the door. "When I'm big," she said, "I'll live in the White House and be the...PRESIDENT!"

Barney drew wheels on his boxes and lined them up in a row. He said, "Someday, I would like to ride across the country on a long train. I could become a...RAILROAD ENGINEER!"

"Oh, Kitty, I love you!" Nell said as she hugged her pet kitten. "You're so cute ...and soft ...and fluffy!

"Kitty, someday I'll take care of many animals. If they get hurt or sick, they can all come to me for help!" Nell said. "I could be a...

VETERINARIAN!"

Barney makes Nell laugh when he does funny tricks. "Someday," Nell said, "you could join a circus and be a...

It was a warm, sunny afternoon and Newton was playing with his sailboat. He said, "Someday, I'll go sailing in a real sailboat and I'll be the...

CAPTAIN!"

Later that afternoon,
Barney saw a movie
on television.
Brave firefighters
fought a large
forest fire.

Barney watched
as a powerful
spray of water
from the hoses
put out the flames.

"That's what I'll be!"
thought Barney.
"Someday, I'll
become a...

FIREFIGHTER!"

"Wow! You go fast!" Nell told her rocking horse. "How exciting it would be to win a real race!

Maybe, that's what I'll be.

Someday I could become a...

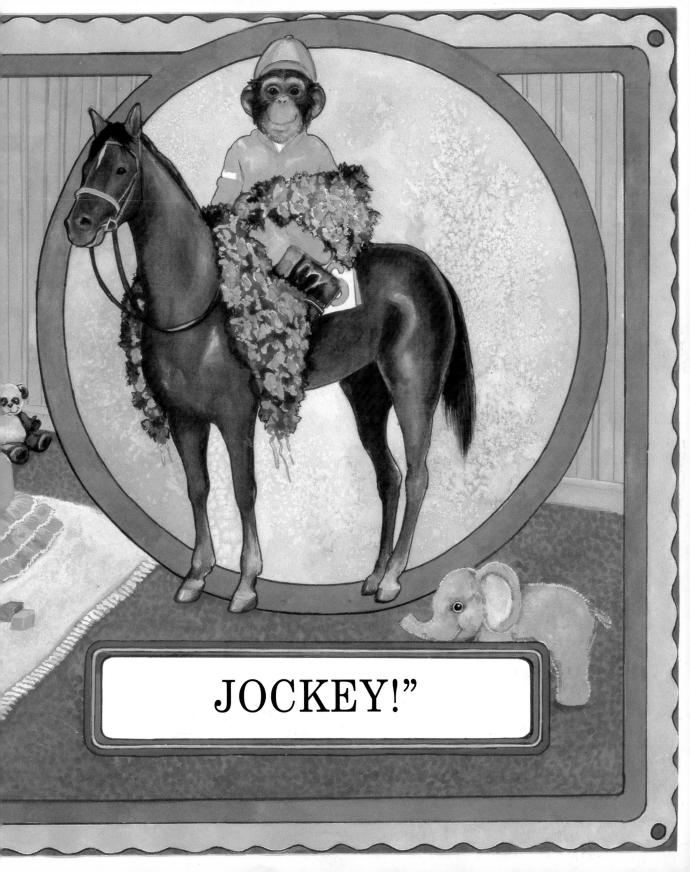

JOCKEY!"

That evening, Newton set his telescope up in the yard. "Come take a look at the craters on the moon!" he told Nell and Barney.

"Every time I look at the sky, I imagine how wonderful it would be to travel in space," Newton said. "Someday I want to be an...

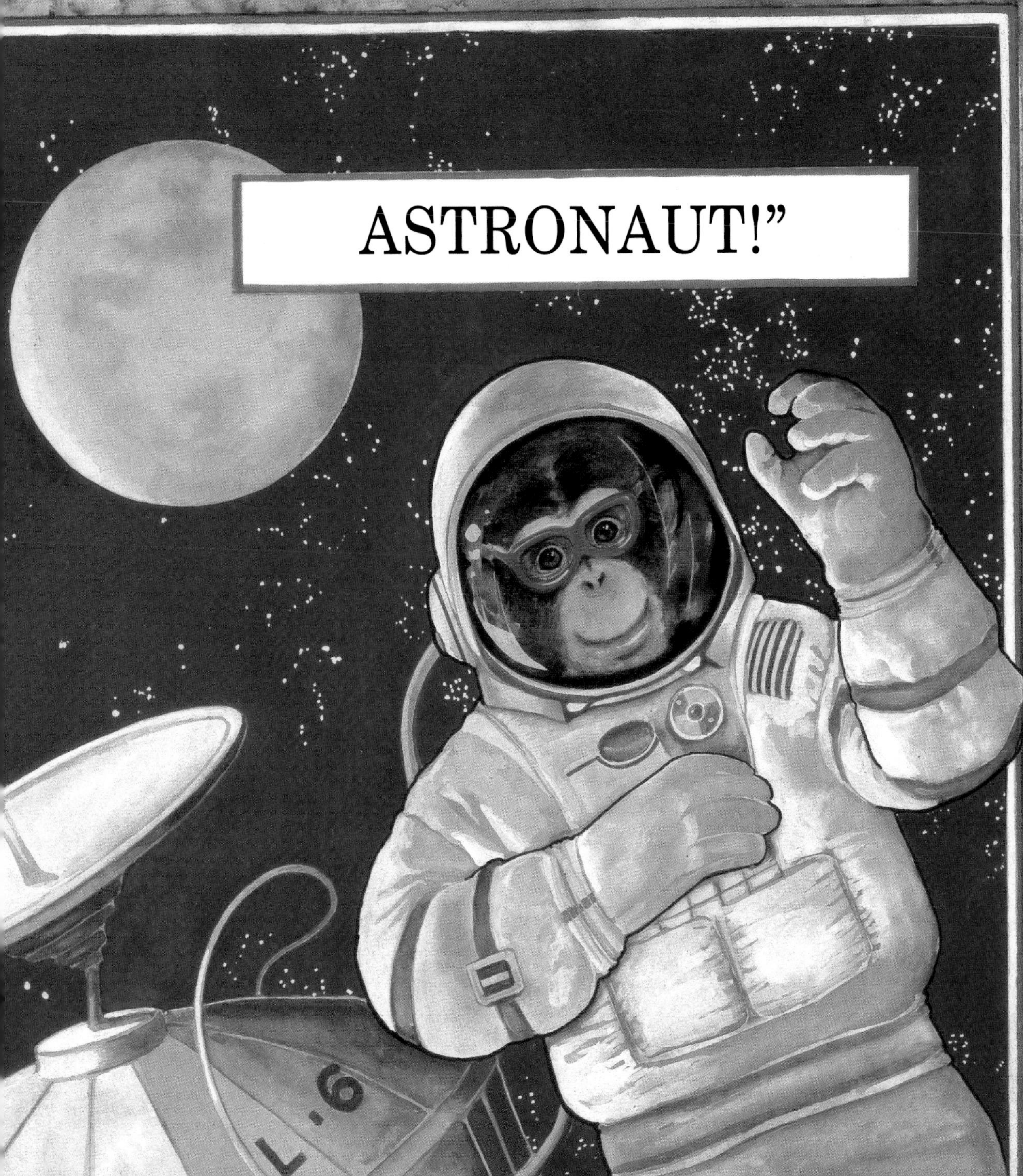

ASTRONAUT!”

During supper, Barney said, "Everytime I play the SOMEDAY game, I change my mind. There are so many good things to be. How will I know which is right for me?"

"Yes, Mama, I'd like to know, too!" Newton added.

"Me too!" Nell joined in.

Mama smiled and said, "In time, you will discover that there are many more things that you enjoy doing. It's too early for you to know which one is perfect for you. Now, it's good just to have fun and play the SOMEDAY game!" Then, Mama put a plate of banana pancakes on the table.

Nell said, "It's been fun playing the SOMEDAY game!"
Newton agreed, "Yes, we can do so many things. Being grown up will be great!"

"You're right!" Barney nodded, sleepily, "but, I'm going to bed now. Tomorrow, we can play again."

The End

All inquiries should be addressed to:
Barron's Educational Series, Inc.
250 Wireless Boulevard
Hauppauge, NY 11788

International Standard Book No. 0-8120-6405-4 (hardcover)
0-8120-1746-3 (paperback)

Library of Congress Catalog Card No. 93-13322

Library of Congress Cataloging-in-Publication Data
Esquinaldo, Virginia
     Newton, Nell, and Barney: someday I want to be — / written and
illustrated by Virginia Esquinaldo.
          p.   cm.
     Summary: Three young chimpanzees imagine some of the different
careers they might choose when they are grown up.
     ISBN 0-8120-6405-4: — ISBN 0-8120-1746-3 (pbk):
     [1. Occupations—Fiction. 2. Imagination—Fiction.
3. Chimpanzees—Fiction.] I. Title.
PZ7.E7467Ne 1993
[E]--dc20   93-13322
                                                                                          CIP
                                                                                            AC

PRINTED IN HONG KONG

3456 9955 98765432